WOW!

BLUE BIRD BIKE

The all new BLUE BIRD BIKE flies faster than any bicycle you can buy. Get rid of your boring old slow bike today and buy the BLUE BIRD BIKE.

PEGGIT

Pegs will hold securely even in the strongest wind. Will not stain clothes or snap and will brighten any clothesline

TICK TOCK

It's always time for a NEW CLOCK!

THE Pram

Your new arrival deserves only the best. Giving anything less just isn't good enough. So, when it comes to choosing a perambulator, the only choice is THE PRAM. Fully sprung to protect from bumps, THE PRAM is the smoothest ride your little one will ever have.

123 BUYITALL STREET
THE CITY

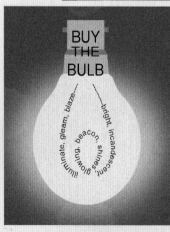

BUY THE BULB

bright, incandescent, shiniest, beacon, glowing, illuminate, gleam, blaze

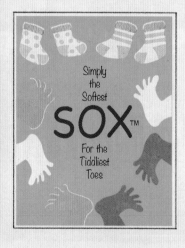

Simply the Softest

SOX™

For the Tiddliest Toes

Too Much
STUFF!

Emily Gravett

TWO HOOTS

In a tree that was taller than all of the rest,
Meg and Ash were busy building a nest.

They built it from mud, and from grass, and from sticks,
And they dreamed that one day they would fill it with chicks.

Then lastly, to keep it all cosy and clean,
They lined the whole thing with an old magazine.

It wasn't that long before they had laid
Four perfect eggs in the nest that they'd made.

But looking around, they worried their nest
Needed more stuff, to make it the best.

And so, while one of them stayed behind,
The other flew off to go and find
The extra things that they agreed
Their chicks were really going to NEED.

At first they brought back little stuff:

Two ornamental cuckoo clocks,
Four tiny socks,
And a pack of plastic pegs
(In shades of blue to match their eggs).

But still it didn't seem enough,
And so . . .

They got some bigger stuff.

A ted abandoned by a bin,
The bin, and EVERYTHING within.

"Better!" they said, "but not quite enough.
Our perfect eggs deserve more stuff."

Meg got some lights for when it got dark.
Ash got a pram from a nearby park.

They nabbed a bucket and a mop
A brush, a broom –
        they could not stop.

They wondered if each chick would like,
To one day learn to ride a bike . . .

And even though it took a while,
The bikes got added to the pile.

After that, they'd NEED a car,
Which may have been a step too far,

As when they went and brought one back
From the nest they heard a . . .

STUFF 1

Down fell the bikes 1, 2, 3, 4,
Quickly followed by much more:

The car came crashing down on top
Followed by the brush and mop.

The shiny bucket, and the lights
Came clattering down from the heights.

The fancy pram that they'd brought back,
Hit the ground with quite a smack.

Falling fast, the poor lost ted
Landed hard upon his head.

On top of him bumped the bin
Its contents now outside (not in).

The clocks came falling mid "cuckoo"
(Just as they were striking two).

And sailing down beside the clocks
Came the pairs of baby socks.

Finally the plastic pegs
Came falling down upon their . . .

"EGGS!"

"Where are our eggs?"

The magpies stopped, and looked around
At all the things strewn on the ground.

And cried: "It didn't seem enough,
But look at all this USELESS STUFF!"

They lifted off the plastic pegs,
But still they couldn't find their eggs.

And so the whole wood set about
Trying to dig their poor nest out.

The lights got pegged up in a tree
So all the animals could see,

The bikes got taken back and left
At the scene of their theft.

The ted was given, by the bugs,
To someone who would give him hugs.

The cuckoo clocks made quite superb
Homes for all the smaller birds.
And the socks made very nice
Cosy beds for baby mice.

The squirrels took the pram apart
And used the bits to make a cart,

The car became a fine fox den
Big enough to hold all ten,

And all the rubbish from the bin
Was swept back up – and put back in.

At last, the magpies reached their nest
(Which was not looking at its best),

"It's just a heap of shell and sticks . . ."

But under that . . .

Four PERFECT chicks!

A CIP catalogue record for this book is available from the British Library • Printed in China • The illustrations in this book were created using watercolour and pencil • www.twohootsbooks.

• 1 3 5 7 9 8 6 4 2 • A CIP catalogue record for this book is available from the British Library

First published 2020 by Two Hoots

This edition published 2021 by Two Hoots an imprint of Pan Macmillan • The Smithson 6 Briset Street London EC1M 5NR • Associated companies throughout the world • www.panmacmillan.com • ISBN 978 1 5098 5735 7

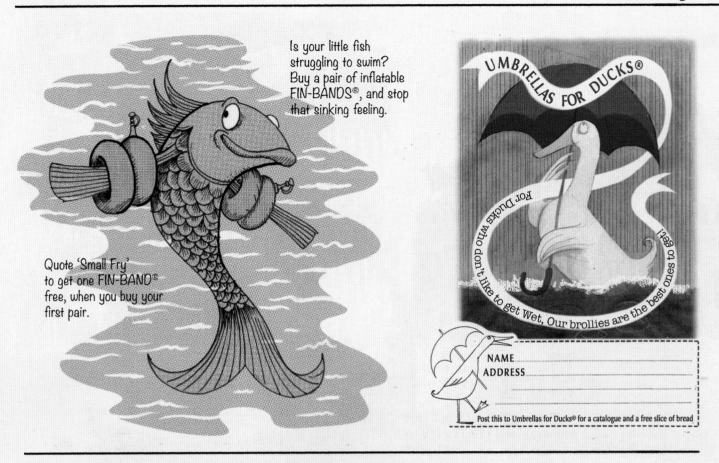
THE FOUR 'R's' of RECYCLING

REDUCE

RE-USE

REPAIR

RECYCLE

MORE BOOKS BY
Emily Gravett

TIDY

Emily Gravett

AGAIN!

Emily Gravett

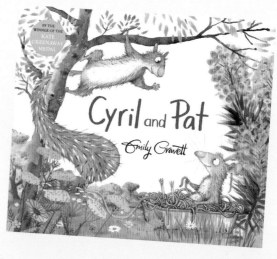

Cyril and Pat

Emily Gravett

WOLVES

Emily Gravett